P9-DDH-256

# Animal Stories

*Retold from the classic originals
by Diane Namm*

*Illustrated by Eric Freeberg*

STERLING

New York / London
**www.sterlingpublishing.com/kids**

STERLING and the distinctive Sterling logo
are registered trademarks of Sterling Publishing Co., Inc.

**Library of Congress Cataloging-in-Publication Data**

Namm, Diane.
  Animal stories / retold from the originals by Diane Namm ; illustrated by
Eric Freeberg.
    v. cm. — (Classic starts)
  Summary: An abridged retelling of a dozen stories about animals from
well-known authors.
  Contents: "Just so" stories / by Rudyard Kipling. How the elephant got his
trunk ; How the camel got his hump ; How the rhinoceros got his skin ; How
the leopard got his spots ; How the whale got his throat ; The beginning of
the armadillos—Stories by Hans Christian Anderson. The leap-frog ; The
wild swans—Dog stories. A dog's tale / by Mark Twain ; Brown wolf / by Jack
London—Stories from "Queer Little Folks" / by Harriet Beecher Stowe. The
squirrels that live in a house ; Mother Magpie's mischief.
  ISBN 978-1-4027-6646-6
  1. Children's stories, American. [1. Short stories. 2. Animals—Fiction.
3. Animals—Folklore. 4. Fairy tales.] I. Freeberg, Eric, ill. II. Title.
  PZ5.N16Ani 2010
  [Fic]—dc22

                                                            2009004839

Lot# :
2  4  6  8  10  9  7  5  3  1
11/09
Published by Sterling Publishing Co., Inc.
387 Park Avenue South, New York, NY 10016
Text © 2010 by Diane Namm
Illustrations © 2010 by Eric Freeberg
Distributed in Canada by Sterling Publishing
$^{c}/o$ Canadian Manda Group, 165 Dufferin Street
Toronto, Ontario, Canada M6K 3H6
Distributed in the United Kingdom by GMC Distribution Services
Castle Place, 166 High Street, Lewes, East Sussex, England BN7 1XU
Distributed in Australia by Capricorn Link (Australia) Pty. Ltd.
P.O. Box 704, Windsor, NSW 2756, Australia

Classic Starts is a trademark of Sterling Publishing Co., Inc.

*Printed in China*
*All rights reserved*

Sterling ISBN 978-1-4027-6646-6

For information about custom editions, special sales, premium and
corporate purchases, please contact Sterling Special Sales
Department at 800-805-5489 or specialsales@sterlingpublishing.com.

# CONTENTS

⁓

### "Just So" Stories
### by Rudyard Kipling

## Stories
### *by Hans Christian Andersen*

## Dog Stories

## Stories from "Queer Little Folks"
### *by Harriet Beecher Stowe*

# "Just So" Stories
## *by Rudyard Kipling*

# CHAPTER 1

# How the Elephant Got His Trunk

Long ago, in far-off times, the Elephant had no trunk. He had only a blackish, bulging nose. It was big as a boot, and he could wriggle it from side to side. But he could not pick up things with it.

There was one Elephant, a new Elephant, named the Elephant's Child. He was full of insatiable curiosity, which means he asked ever so many questions. He lived in Africa. He bothered all of Africa with his questions.

He asked his tall aunt, the Ostrich, why her

tail feathers grew just so. Ostrich bopped him with her hard, hard claw. He asked his tall uncle, the Giraffe, what made his skin so spotty. Giraffe bopped him with his hard, hard hoof.

Still the Elephant's Child was curious. He asked his broad aunt, the Hippopotamus, why her eyes were red. Hippopotamus bopped him with her broad, broad hoof. He asked his hairy uncle, the Baboon, why melons tasted just so. Baboon bopped him with his hairy, hairy paw. And still Elephant's Child was curious.

He asked questions about everything he saw, or heard, or felt, or smelled, or touched. All of his uncles and his aunts bopped him. And still he was full of 'satiable curiosity!

One fine morning, in the middle of a great parade, the Elephant's Child thought of a brand-new question.

"What does the Crocodile have for dinner?" he asked.

"Hush!" everyone hissed in a dreadful tone. Then they bopped him and bopped him for a good long time until he was very warm and greatly surprised.

The Elephant's Child ran off crying into the jungle. He came upon a Kolokolo Bird sitting in the middle of a thorn bush.

"Why are you crying?" asked the Kolokolo Bird.

"Everyone has bopped me for my 'satiable curiosity. But I still want to know what the Crocodile has for dinner!"

"Go to the banks of the great gray-green, greasy Limpopo River. You'll find out there," the Kolokolo Bird told him.

That next day, the Elephant's Child took a hundred pounds of bananas (the short red kind), and a hundred pounds of sugarcane (the long purple kind), and seventeen melons (the green crackly kind). He carried them in a sack.

"Good-bye, dear family. I am going to the great gray-green, greasy Limpopo River. I must find out what the Crocodile has for dinner," he said.

They all bopped him once more, for luck, even though he most politely asked them to stop.

The Elephant's Child went from town to town and county to county. All the way, he ate melons and left the rinds (because he could not pick them up). He traveled for many days and many nights. At last he came to the great gray-green, greasy Limpopo River. The first thing he found was a two-colored Python-Rock-Snake curled around a rock.

"Excuse me," said the Elephant's Child. "Have you seen such a thing as a Crocodile? And do you know what he has for dinner?"

The two-colored Python-Rock-Snake uncoiled himself from the rock. He bopped the Elephant's Child with his scalesome, flailsome tail.

"Why does everyone bop me for my 'satiable curiosity?" the Elephant's Child wondered.

Now he was more determined than ever to find out what the Crocodile eats for dinner. So the Elephant's Child went right up to the great gray-green, greasy Limpopo River and sat down on a log.

But it was not a log. It was really the Crocodile. The Elephant's Child did not know this. And the Crocodile winked one eye at the Elephant's Child.

"Did you happen to see a Crocodile near the great gray-green, greasy Limpopo River?" asked the Elephant's Child most politely.

The Crocodile winked the other eye. He lifted his tail out of the mud. The Elephant's Child stood up and stepped back. He did not wish to be bopped again.

"Come here, little one," said the Crocodile. "Why do you ask such things?"

"Excuse me," said the Elephant's Child, eyeing the Crocodile's tail. "I have been bopped by my father, my mother, my tall aunt, my tall uncle, my broad aunt, my hairy uncle, *and* the two-colored Python-Rock-Snake. All because I want to know what the Crocodile has for dinner. But I do *not* want to be bopped anymore."

"Come closer, little one," said the Crocodile. "I am the Crocodile you are looking for." He wept crocodile tears to show it was true.

The Elephant's Child kneeled down beside the riverbank. "Will you please, please tell me what you have for dinner?" he asked with excitement.

"Come closer still, little one, and I'll whisper it to you," the Crocodile said.

Then the Elephant's Child put his head down close to the Crocodile's musky, tusky mouth. The Crocodile caught him by his little blackish, bulging nose, which up until that moment had been no bigger than a boot.

"I think," the Crocodile hissed between his teeth, "that today my dinner shall be the Elephant's Child!"

"Let go! You are hurting me!" the Elephant Child cried. Just then the two-colored Python-Rock-Snake slithered down from the bank. He whispered into the Elephant Child's ear.

"Young friend, you must pull as hard as you can—immediately and at once! Or else the Crocodile will eat you up," the two-colored Python-Rock-Snake advised.

So the Elephant's Child sat back on his little hind legs. He pulled and he pulled and he pulled. His nose began to stretch. Then the Crocodile swished his mighty tail and he pulled and he pulled and he pulled. The Elephant's Child's nose kept on stretching and stretching! Now his nose was nearly five feet long!

Just then the two-colored Python-Rock-Snake knotted himself around the Elephant's

Child's back legs. He pulled and the Elephant's Child pulled and the Crocodile pulled the other way. But the Elephant's Child and the Python-Rock-Snake pulled the hardest. At last the Crocodile let go of the Elephant's Child's nose. It dropped with a thud that could be heard all up and down the great gray-green, greasy Limpopo River.

"Oh, no," cried the Elephant's Child. "My nose is ruined!"

"Some people do not know a good thing when it is as plain as the nose on their faces!" said the two-colored Python-Rock-Snake.

At first, the Elephant's Child did not know what the two-colored Python-Rock-Snake meant. But then a bee stung him on his shoulder. Before he knew what he was doing, the Elephant's Child used his trunk to swat the bee away.

"See? You couldn't have done that with

a mere-smear nose," said the Python-Rock-Snake.

"That's true," realized the Elephant's Child. Then, with his new nose, he plucked a large bundle of grass from the ground and stuffed it into his mouth.

"See? You couldn't have done that with a mere-smear nose," the Python-Rock-Snake pointed out.

"True again," said the Elephant's Child as he

chewed on the sweet bundle of grass in the hot jungle sun.

Before he realized what he was doing, the Elephant's Child scooped up a great big glob of mud from the banks of the great gray-green, greasy Limpopo River. He slapped it on his head. It made a cool, sloshy mud cap that trickled down behind his ears.

"Oooh, that feels good," the Elephant's Child said.

"See? You couldn't have done that with a mere-smear nose. Now, how do you feel about being bopped again?"

"I should not like that at all," said the Elephant's Child, raising his very long and stretched-out nose in the air.

"Well, you will find that your brand-new nose will be very useful to defend yourself with," the two-colored Python-Rock-Snake said.

So the Elephant's Child went home across

Africa, flapping and waving his trunk along the way. He was careful to pick up all the melon rinds he had tossed on his trip to the great gray-green, greasy Limpopo River. After all, he *was* a tidy Elephant's Child.

When the Elephant's Child got home, everyone told him how ugly his new nose looked. They wanted to bop him again for his 'satiable curiosity. The Elephant's Child had had enough. He bopped all his dear family for a very long time until they were very warm and greatly surprised.

The rest of the family was so jealous of the Elephant's Child. They now wanted noses like his, for bopping. So they each went off in a great hurry to the banks of the great gray-green, greasy Limpopo River so the Crocodile could give them new noses, too.

And that is how the Elephant got his trunk!

CHAPTER 2

# How the Camel Got His Hump

༺ঌ

This next tale tells of how the Camel got his big hump.

In the beginning of years, when the world was very new, there was a Camel who lived in the middle of a Howling Desert. He did not like to work. He ate sticks and thorns and milkweed and prickles. Whenever anyone spoke to him, all he said was "Humph!" and nothing more.

One morning, the Horse, Dog, and Ox came to him. The Horse said, "Oh, Camel. Come work with us and Man to make the Desert a better place."

But the Camel just said, "Humph!"

The Dog came to the Camel and said, "Oh, Camel. Come work with us and Man to make the Desert a better place."

But the Camel just said, "Humph!"

The Ox came to the Camel and said, "Oh, Camel. Come work with us and Man to make the Desert a better place."

Again, the Camel just said, "Humph!"

Then the Man, Horse, Dog, and Ox had a meeting. "It is a shame that the Camel will not work to help us make the Desert a better place. But since he will not, we must all work twice as hard to make up for it," the Man said.

For three long days, the Man, Horse, Dog, and Ox worked very hard in the Desert. The Camel came to watch. He chewed on his milkweed and laughed at them while they worked and sweated in the hot desert sun. This made the Horse, Dog, and Ox very angry.

On the third night, while the Man slept, the Horse, Dog, and Ox were too upset to sleep. They talked about how they could make the Camel work. Just then a Magic Genie came across the Howling Desert in a cloud of dust. The Horse offered him some food. The Dog offered him a cool cup of water. The Ox offered him a bed of hay in which to rest.

"You are all so kind to me," said the Genie. "What can I do for you?" he asked.

"For three days, we have worked ourselves to the bone," began the Horse.

"But the Camel, who also lives in the Howling Desert, will not help," said the Dog.

"All he does is laugh at us and say, 'Humph,'" added the Ox.

"Don't worry," said the Magic Genie. "I will talk to him." So the Magic Genie went to visit the Camel.

"The Horse, Dog, and Ox are working very

hard," said the Magic Genie to the Camel, but all the Camel replied was "Humph!"

"They are working very hard to make our Desert a better place," the Magic Genie explained.

"Humph!" the Camel said again.

"I wouldn't say that again if I were you," the Magic Genie warned him. "Now, you have missed three days of work. When the sun comes up, I want you to help them with their work."

"Humph!" was all the Camel would say.

"I warned you!" the Magic Genie replied. Then with a swoosh of his hand, he raised a terrible twirling, twisting cloud of dust. The Camel's back began to puff up and up. When the dust cleared, the Camel had a great big lolloping humph—right on top of his back!

"See what you've done," the Magic Genie scolded. "That's your very own humph. You've brought it on yourself. And now you will get to work at once. You will work for three days straight to make up for the days you've missed," ordered the Magic Genie.

"But how can I?" bleated the Camel. "I cannot go without food and drink for three long days."

"Ah, but you can," the Magic Genie assured him. "You can store food and water in the humph on your back. That way you can work for three days without stopping to eat or drink. You can live on your humph while you work. And you will spend the rest of your days working alongside the Man, Horse, Dog, and Ox to make the Desert a better place."

The Genie was gone in another terrible, twisting, twirling cloud of dust. And that is how the Camel got his hump (which is what we call it instead of Humph!).

# CHAPTER 3

# How the Rhinoceros Got His Skin

∽

Once upon a time there lived a magician called the Parsee. He lived on an island all by himself on the shores of the Red Sea. He had nothing but his sun hat, his knife, and a cooking stove.

One day he took flour, water, currants, plums, and sugar. He mixed them all together and baked them on his stove. He made a splendid cake that was two feet across and three feet thick.

"What is that delicious smell?" wondered the Rhinoceros, who followed his nose all the way down to the beach.

In those days the Rhinoceros had a horn on his nose, two piggy eyes, and a skin-coat of which he was most proud. His skin-coat fit tight on his body. There was not a wrinkle to be found on the Rhinoceros's skin. Not only was the Rhinoceros a very proud beast, but he was also very rude. When he followed his nose to the Parsee's camp, he saw the splendid cake.

"I must have that cake!" the Rhinoceros decided.

Just as the Parsee was about to take a bite of his splendid cake, the Rhinoceros made a run to grab it. The Parsee scrambled up a palm tree, quick as a wink, to avoid being trampled. The Rhinoceros knocked over the Parsee's precious stove. The splendid cake rolled into the sand. At once, the Rhinoceros speared it with his horn. Then he ran off, gobbling the cake as he ran, waving his tail at the poor, hungry Parsee.

When the Parsee climbed down from the palm tree, he was very angry with the Rhinoceros. He chanted to himself,

> Them that takes the cakes
>
> Which the Parsee man bakes
>
> Makes dreadful mistakes.

Several weeks later, there was a terrible heat wave on the island. The Parsee and all the animals took off all their clothes to stay cool. The Parsee took off his magnificent hat. And the Rhinoceros took off his very tight skin.

Very carefully, so he would not wrinkle it a bit, the Rhinoceros unbuttoned the three buttons that held his skin together. Very, very carefully, he neatly folded his skin and laid it down beside the water. Then the Rhinoceros waddled into the water and blew bubbles through his nose. He paid no attention to the Parsee. Not even to apologize for ruining his stove. Not even to thank him for the splendid cake he had taken from him.

While the Rhinoceros cooled himself in the water, the Parsee went to work. He went back to his camp and filled his splendid hat with crumbs and currants. He crept over to the Rhinoceros's neatly folded skin. Next he scrubbed and rubbed that skin with old, dry, stale, tickly cake-crumbs and lots of burnt currants (the Parsee always ate cake and had lots of leftover crumbs).

Then the Parsee scampered up the palm tree to wait for the Rhinoceros to put on his skin.

As soon as the Rhinoceros buttoned up his skin, he began to itch. His skin tickled and bothered and crawled. First he tried to scratch, but that just made it worse. Then he lay down on the sand and rolled and rolled, but that made it even worse than before. Next, he ran to the palm tree and rubbed and rubbed and rubbed his skin against it as hard as he could. He rubbed his three buttons right off! He rubbed so hard that his skin stretched into great big folds on his shoulders, stomach, and legs.

But this did him no good. No matter how much he scratched, rolled, and rubbed, the cake-crumbs made him itchier than before. He went home angry, itchy, and very, very wrinkled.

That is why the Rhinoceros has a very bad temper, and why he has such great wrinkles and folds in his skin!

# CHAPTER 4

# How the Leopard Got His Spots

ᴄᴏ

In the days when all creatures roamed the golden grassy fields of Africa, the Leopard and the Warrior-Man would hunt the Giraffe and the Zebra, and sometimes other animals, too. The Leopard and the Warrior were so good at hunting that the Giraffe and the Zebra never knew when they were there. They were so worried all the time that they could never sleep.

One day, the Giraffe and the Zebra decided to leave the grassy fields. They went to live in a great forest filled with trees and bushes that cast stripy, speckly, patchy-blatchy shadows where they could hide. They lived there safely for many seasons, standing half in the shade and half in the sun. In fact, they stood for so long in the slippery-slidy shadows of the great forest that the Giraffe became spotted and the Zebra became striped. For a very long time they led beautiful lives in the speckly-spickly, uneven shadows of the forest.

However, the Leopard and the Warrior were not having beautiful lives in the tall yellow-green grass fields. They were hungry because there were no more Giraffes and Zebras left to hunt. So they went to visit the Wisest Animal in all of South Africa, the dog-headed barking Baboon.

"Where have the Giraffes and Zebras all gone?" asked the Leopard and the Warrior.

"They have gone to other spots. My advice to you, Leopard, is to go to other spots as soon as you can," said the Baboon with a wink. And then he said no more.

Puzzled, the Leopard and the Warrior set off in search of other spots. They came to the great, tall forest that was speckled and spotted, and slashed and splashed and hatched and thatched with shadows.

"We are wasting our time here," said the Leopard. "There is nothing but shadows."

"Wait a moment," said the Warrior. "I can smell the Giraffe. I can hear the Giraffe. I just can't see the Giraffe."

The Leopard sniffed the shadowy air and listened to the breeze. "I can smell the Zebra. I can hear the Zebra. I just can't see the Zebra," he declared.

So they hunted the Giraffe and the Zebra all day. Although they could smell them and hear them, they still couldn't see them.

Then it grew dark. The Leopard heard something breathing heavily in the starlight. It smelled like the Zebra. It sounded like the Zebra. So he pounced and knocked it down to the ground. It kicked like the Zebra. But he still couldn't see what it was!

"I am going to sit on your head until morning when I can see you," the Leopard growled. "Then I will know what you are."

Just then, the Leopard heard a crash and a scramble. The Warrior called out, "I've caught something. It smells like the Giraffe. It sounds like the Giraffe, and it kicks like the Giraffe, but I can't see it!"

"Sit on its head till morning," answered the Leopard. "Then we can sort it all out."

In the morning when the light appeared, the Leopard and the Warrior still couldn't figure out what they had caught. Neither the Giraffe nor the Zebra looked the way they had when they lived in the tall, high yellow grass fields.

"What kind of creatures are you?" the Leopard growled.

"Let us up," the Zebra said.

"Then we'll tell you," offered the Giraffe.

So the Warrior and the Leopard released the creatures.

"Now watch," said the Zebra and the Giraffe. "One, two, three!"

At once, the Zebra moved away into the thorn bushes where the shadows were stripy. The Giraffe moved off to some tall trees where the shadows fell on him in blotchy patterns.

"And now where are we?" asked a voice from the shadows.

The Leopard and the Warrior stared and stared. But they could see no signs of the Zebra and the Giraffe.

The Warrior turned to the Leopard and said, "This is a trick worth learning. We will never catch our dinner again unless we hide ourselves in the stripy shadows of the forest."

At once, the Warrior began to blacken his skin with blackish brown mud.

"What about me?" asked the Leopard.

"I'll give you spots," said the Warrior.

He pressed his fingers into the blackish brown mud and smeared it all over the Leopard's fur coat. Then he stepped back to take a look.

"Now you are a beauty," said the Warrior. "You can lie out on the bare ground and look like a heap of pebbles. You can lie out on the open rocks and look like a piece of stone. You can lie out on a leafy branch and look like sunshine sifting through the leaves. And you can lie right across the center of a path and look like nothing at all. Think of that and purr!"

From that day on, the Leopard and the Warrior were able to hide and hunt happily in the forest.

And that is how the Leopard got his spots!

CHAPTER 5

# How the Whale Got His Throat

∽

Once upon a time, in the sea, there was a Whale. He ate fish and other creatures of every size. He ate starfish and garfish. He ate crab and dab, mackerel and pickerel, and the truly twirly-whirly eel.

All the underwater creatures were worried that the Whale would eat every little fish in the sea! They came up with a plan. They sent the littlest fish, the "Stute" Fish, who could swim beside the Whale's ear, to speak with him. If he could convince the Whale to eat people, perhaps he would leave the fish in the sea alone.

"Noble and generous Sir Whale. Have you ever tasted Man? He's quite delicious," said the "Stute" Fish.

"Where would I find this Man?" the Whale asked, since he was starting to feel hungry again.

"Follow me," said the littlest "Stute" Fish.

They swam as fast and as far as they could until they came to a raft in the middle of the sea. There they found a shipwrecked Sailor. He had nothing but a pair of blue jeans, suspenders, and a jackknife.

When the Whale spotted the Sailor, he opened his mouth wide. He swallowed him whole, including his raft, blue jeans, suspenders, and jackknife. Then the Whale smacked his lips and made three circles with his tail.

As soon as the Sailor was inside the Whale's

warm, dark insides, he thumped and bumped. He pranced and danced. He banged and clanged. He hit and bit, he leaped and creeped, he prowled and howled, he hopped and dropped. Then he cried and sighed, crawled and bawled, and played music to make himself feel better. The Whale was most unhappy about all the noise!

He called down his throat to the Sailor. "Come out and behave yourself. You're giving me the hiccups," he said.

"I will not come out! Take me home to my family and I will think about it," answered the clever Sailor. Then he began to dance.

The Whale swam as fast as he could, in spite of his hiccups. While the Whale swam, the Sailor thought to himself, "If the Whale can eat me, he can eat other people, too. I have to stop him."

While the Whale swam, the Sailor got to work. He cut up his raft with his jackknife. He tied the pieces together with his suspenders to make a crisscross grate. Then the Sailor stuck the crisscross grate behind him and into the back of the Whale's huge throat.

When at last the Whale brought the Sailor home, he stepped out of the great big mouth happily onto the shore. He thanked the Whale for his ride home. Then he turned and left.

From that day on, the Whale had a crisscross grate in his throat. It was fixed so tight that he could not swallow it up or cough it out. To eat, the Whale could now only swallow the tiniest fish in the sea, and would never again eat a man, woman, or child.

This is how the Whale got his throat. (And the little "Stute" Fish now hides in the mud so that the Whale can never find him!)

# CHAPTER 6

# The Beginning of the Armadillos

 ∽

In olden days, on the banks of the wild and dangerous Amazon River, there lived two very good friends. One was Stickly-Prickly Hedgehog who ate shelled snails and things. The other was Slow-and-Solid Tortoise who ate green lettuces and things.

Painted Jaguar, who ate anything he could catch, also lived along the banks of the Amazon River. When he could not catch deer or monkeys, he would catch frogs and beetles. When there were no more deer, monkeys, frogs, or beetles left, he asked his mother what else he should catch.

"Hedgehogs and Tortoises," she said. "To catch a Hedgehog, drop him into the water. He'll uncoil, and then you can eat him. To catch a Tortoise, scoop him out of his shell with your paw."

One beautiful night along the banks of the wild and dangerous Amazon River, Painted Jaguar found Stickly-Prickly Hedgehog and Slow-and-Solid Tortoise. In defense, Stickly-Prickly Hedgehog curled himself into a ball. Slow-and-Solid Tortoise drew his head and feet into his shell. But Painted Jaguar didn't care.

"Which one of you is a Hedgehog, and which one of you is a Tortoise?" he asked.

"Why do you want to know?" asked Slow-and-Solid Tortoise from inside his shell.

Painted Jaguar explained about his mother's advice.

"I think your mother is all mixed up," said Stickly-Prickly. "The truth is, when you uncoil a Tortoise, you should scoop him out of the water."

"And when you paw a Hedgehog, you must drop him on his shell," added Slow-and-Solid Tortoise.

"Or perhaps when you water a Hedgehog you must drop him into your paw," said Stickly-Prickly Hedgehog.

"Or when you meet a Tortoise you must shell him until he uncoils," said Slow-and-Solid Tortoise.

"Stop! You make my spots ache. I don't want your advice at all. I just want to know which of you is which," cried Painted Jaguar.

"I'm not telling you," said Stickly-Prickly Hedgehog. "Just try scooping me out of my shell."

"Aha!" said Painted Jaguar. "So you're the

Tortoise!" Painted Jaguar reached for Stickly-Prickly Hedgehog just as he curled himself up into a ball.

"Ow!" said Painted Jaguar. He felt a sting as he knocked Stickly-Prickly Hedgehog deep into the bushes. His paw was full of prickles. Then he turned to Slow-and-Solid Tortoise.

"So you must be a Tortoise!" Painted Jaguar said, nursing his prickly paw in his mouth. "I'll just scoop you out of your shell."

"Are you sure that's what your mother said?" asked Slow-and-Solid Tortoise. "I thought she told you to drop me into the water and then scoop me out of my shell."

Painted Jaguar thought a moment. He couldn't remember what his mother had said. "Now I'm all mixed up," he said.

"You seem quite anxious for me to drop you into the water. That makes me think you really don't want to be. Which means, that's exactly what I'll do!" cried Painted Jaguar as he dropped Slow-and-Solid Tortoise into the river.

As soon as Slow-and-Solid Tortoise hit the water, he swam away as fast as he could.

"They got away!" Painted Jaguar told his mother as he explained what had happened that day.

Meanwhile, Stickly-Prickly Hedgehog and Slow-and-Solid Tortoise knew that Painted Jaguar would be back. So they came up with a new and clever plan. Slow-and-Solid Tortoise taught Stickly-Prickly Hedgehog how to swim. Stickly-Prickly Hedgehog loosened Slow-and-Solid Tortoise's back shell plates so he could curl up in a ball. As they each practiced curling up and swimming, a curious thing occurred. Slow-and-Solid Tortoise's back plates started to overlap instead of lying side by side. And Stickly-Prickly Hedgehog's prickles began to blend together.

After several days of practicing each other's

moves, they looked very similar. In fact, they looked nothing like what they were before. They gazed at their reflections in the water of the wild and dangerous Amazon River.

"We will certainly confuse Painted Jaguar now," they laughed together. "Let's go find him."

They came upon Painted Jaguar, still nursing his prickly paw.

"Good morning," said Stickly-Prickly Hedgehog.

"How is your mother?" asked Slow-and-Solid Tortoise.

"Who are you?" asked Painted Jaguar. "And how do you know my mother?"

"Don't you remember us?" asked Stickly-Prickly Hedgehog.

"Hedgehog and Tortoise," Slow-and-Solid Tortoise reminded him.

"Aha!" said Painted Jaguar. He reached out to grab them.

They both curled themselves up and rolled

around Painted Jaguar until his eyes turned cartwheels in his head. Then they rolled off to safety in the woods while Painted Jaguar went to find his mother.

"But it wasn't exactly a Hedgehog, and it wasn't precisely a Tortoise," Painted Jaguar tried to explain.

"Then we shall call it an Armadillo," said Painted Jaguar's mother, "until we can give it a proper name."

And from that day to this, the swimming Hedgehog with the prickly coat and the curling Tortoise with the overlapping shell are known as the Armadillo!

# Stories

*by Hans Christian Andersen*

# CHAPTER 7

# The Leap-Frog

Once upon a time, when animals and people spoke to each other as equals, a Flea, a Grasshopper, and a Leap-Frog wanted to see who could jump the highest. These three famous jumpers invited the whole world to a festival in which they would compete.

Upon hearing of this festival, the King offered his daughter's hand in marriage to the winner of the competition. "I will marry the Princess to the one who can jump the highest," the King declared. "A contest is only as good as its reward, and my daughter is most precious to me."

The Flea stepped forward first to present himself to the King and the Princess.

"It is my greatest pleasure, Your Highnesses, to serve you in any way I can," said the Flea with a noble bow of his head. Then he turned, faced the crowd, and waved to the people as if he were already part of the royal family.

Next was the Grasshopper. He wore a green uniform, which was a sign of his family's military tradition. He, too, bowed low before the King and the Princess. He sang his own praises rather loudly. "I am the brightest and most handsome of creatures," Grasshopper told them.

Both the Flea and the Grasshopper were quite sure that they were each good enough to marry a Princess. They were each quite sure that they would win.

In contrast with his bragging challengers, the Leap-Frog said nothing. But that doesn't mean nothing was said about him. Actually, the people had a great deal to say about the Leap-Frog.

"He is definitely from a good and noble family," said the Royal Dog.

"I believe he may be a prophet of some sort," said the Old Royal Counselor. "Look at the Leap-Frog's back. We can predict if the coming winter will be harsh or mild just from its color," he added.

"He has quite a royal expression," murmured someone in the crowd.

"Silence!" ordered the King. "Keep your thoughts to yourselves until the contest is won."

The drums rolled. The trumpets sounded. The crowd clapped and cheered. The Flea, the Grasshopper, and the Leap-Frog all mounted the jumping platform.

"First jumper!" called the Royal Page.

The Flea bowed again to the King and the
crowd. He crouched lower than low on his little
flea knees.

"Here . . . I . . . go!" he called out. Then the
Flea jumped high in the sky.

"Where did he go?" the crowd wondered.
The Flea was nowhere in sight.

"Disqualified!" declared the Royal Judge. "Since the Flea cannot be seen, it is clear he did not jump. He is a dishonorable contestant. Disqualified, I say!" he repeated.

"Second jumper!" announced the Royal Page.

The Grasshopper rubbed his legs together and chirped, "One, two, three. Look at me!"

The Grasshopper jumped into the air and landed . . . right on the King's face. The King was so surprised, he fell right off his throne!

"Ill-mannered!" declared the Royal Judge. Then he helped the King back into his seat. "Impolite insect!" the Royal Judge muttered to himself.

At last it was the Leap-Frog's turn. The drums rolled. The trumpets sounded. The crowd clapped and cheered. But the Leap-Frog didn't move.

"Is he ill?" the Royal Dog asked.

"Is he afraid?" the crowd began to wonder.

"Will he never jump?" the Royal Judge thundered.

But then, quick as lightning, the Leap-Frog went *pop!* He didn't jump up. He didn't jump forward. He jumped sideways, right into . . . the Princess's lap. Leap-Frog jumped so gently and in such a gentlemanly way that the pretty Princess did not budge from her golden stool.

"Leap-Frog is the winner!" the King declared.

"But I jumped much higher," the Grasshopper cried.

"I jumped the highest!" shouted the Flea.

"The Leap-Frog knows there is nothing in this world that I hold higher than my daughter. To jump to her is to make the highest jump there is. Leap-Frog is a wise fellow. He shall have my daughter's hand," announced the King.

"She may have the old Leap-Frog for all I care. In this world, the best man never receives his rightful reward," said the Flea. He then marched off to join the Foreign Service and was never, ever heard from again.

"I will never understand this," the Grasshopper said sadly. He hopped off to a green riverbank to think about things.

Rubbing his legs together, he chirped a sorrowful song that told the story of how the Leap-Frog won the jumping contest. He may still be there, chirping his song.

And the Leap-Frog and the Princess lived together with the King—happily ever after, of course!

# CHAPTER 8

# The Wild Swans

Far away, in a land where swallows fly in winter, lived a king who had eleven sons and one daughter, named Eliza. The eleven brothers were princes. Each prince went to school with a star on his chest and a sword at his side. They wrote with diamond pencils on golden slates. They learned their lessons quickly and read quite easily, as princes are likely to do.

While the princes were at school, Princess Eliza sat on a little glass stool and studied a book of pictures. The book was so precious, it cost as much as a half a kingdom.

These were happy days for the royal family. But one day, the king married a wicked queen. She did not love the king's children at all.

During the wedding party, the wicked queen made sure that everyone else in the land had plenty of cakes and apples. But when she turned to the king's children, she gave them tiny bowls filled with sand and told them to pretend it was cake.

One week after the wedding, the wicked queen sent Princess Eliza to live with a peasant and his wife. She told the king many lies about the young princes. The king believed her and no longer cared for his sons.

The princes tried to convince their father that the wicked queen had enchanted him. But the king would not listen to them. Then the wicked queen put a curse on the eleven handsome princes.

"Go out into the world and leave us alone," she told them. "Fly like great birds that have no voice and forever roam the skies. You will be princes no longer!"

Although the wicked queen's plan was to turn them into ugly birds of prey, her magic didn't work. Instead the princes turned into eleven beautiful wild swans. All at once they flew through the windows of the palace, over the kingdom, to the forest beyond. They hovered over the peasant cottage where their sister, Princess Eliza, had been sent. She did not see them. They had no voices so they could not speak to her and tell her of the wicked queen's curse. So they flew far away and took shelter in a cave in a thick, dark wood. They were far away from their kingdom and from the wicked queen.

Princess Eliza spent four long years in the peasant cottage. She had no toys and no friends.

She had no one to read her stories and tuck her in at night, as her brothers had always done. She had no one to give her kisses and hugs, the way her brothers had. One day passed like another, until she turned fifteen. The king became curious and asked to see his daughter, which greatly upset the wicked queen. But the king insisted, and Eliza was brought to the palace at once.

The wicked queen was distressed at the sight of Eliza's beauty and goodness. She was sick at heart to think that the king would want Eliza to come back to the palace. So the wicked queen came up with an evil plan. She would use her magic to disguise Eliza so the king would not recognize her.

The wicked queen conjured up three toads to do her evil chore. She kissed the toads and put a spell on each one.

"Now, my lovely, here's what you must do," the wicked queen told the first toad. "Sit on

Princess Eliza's head so that she may become as stupid as you are."

The wicked queen said to the second toad, "Sit on Eliza's fair cheek so that she may become as ugly as you. Then her father will not recognize her and will turn her away."

To the third toad, the wicked queen whispered, "Rest on her heart so she will become evil. Then her father will not love her."

When Eliza returned for her first night back at the palace, the wicked queen placed all three toads in her bath. She told the princess to clean up and get ready for bed.

"Your father will want to see you fresh and bright tomorrow morning," the wicked queen said.

As Eliza lowered herself into the bath, she did not notice the ugly toads. Minutes later, when she rose from her bath, she noticed three red poppies floating in the tub. The toads had been turned into flowers. Princess Eliza was too good and innocent for the wicked queen's witchcraft to have any effect on her at all! She went to sleep, as beautiful and kind as ever.

The wicked queen was furious. She had to do something quickly. While Eliza slept, the wicked queen rubbed walnut juice all over her until she was quite brown. Then she tangled Eliza's beautiful hair and smeared it with disgusting ointment.

"Your father will never recognize you now, Princess," the wicked queen chuckled to herself.

The next day, the king called for his daughter. Eliza politely stood before her father and bowed.

"Who is this little brown troll?" roared the king. "And what have you done with my beautiful daughter Eliza?"

"Father, it's me. Don't you remember?" Eliza cried.

"Have this fake thrown out of the palace," the king demanded. "Send out a search party for my daughter. If anyone harms a hair on her head, I will punish them!"

Eliza was tossed out of the palace grounds. She wept as she stumbled down the path that led away from the palace. She missed her eleven brothers. She knew that if she could find them, they would recognize her at once and set things right with the king.

Not knowing which direction to walk, Eliza set forth over fields and meadows. She came to a great forest. It was quickly becoming night, and she didn't want to wander in the dark forest. She lay down on the soft mossy ground and offered up an evening prayer to the moon above. The soft night air cooled her forehead. The light of hundreds of glowworms shone in the grass and moss. The brilliant insects glowed around her like shooting stars.

All night long, Eliza dreamed of her brothers.
She imagined they were all children again, playing
together. She saw them writing with their diamond pencils on golden slates. She remembered
looking at her beautiful picture book, which had
cost half a kingdom. Only in her dream, the
pages of the picture book contained stories of

the noble deeds she and her brothers would perform once they were reunited.

When Eliza woke up, the sun was high. Slivers of sunlight glimmered through the thick branches overhead. She peered through the golden mist. There was a sweet smell of fresh grass, and birds were flying among the branches. She heard the cool rippling of water in a lake nearby. Eliza followed the trail of a deer's hoof-prints to the water below.

The lake water was so clear that it looked like a painting on the ground. Every leaf from the surrounding trees was reflected in the water. Eliza looked down and saw her reflection. Her soiled face and rumpled hair made her jump in surprise. When she realized it was her very own face that had startled her, she immediately jumped in the lake to bathe. She emerged fresh and clean—once again the beautiful Princess Eliza.

Determined to find her brothers, Eliza set out

again through the forest, looking for clues about where they might be. She found none. She was afraid she might never again find her brothers, or a safe place to be.

Sorrowfully, she lay herself down to sleep. She was very tired from searching all day.

The next morning, an old woman was out berry-picking and found Eliza sleeping at the foot of a tree.

"Wake up, child," the old woman said, shaking Eliza gently. "What are you doing sleeping alone in the forest?" Eliza explained that she was looking for her eleven princely brothers.

"Have you seen them?" Eliza asked, her voice full of hope.

"I haven't seen eleven men. But just yesterday I saw eleven swans, with gold crowns on their heads, swimming down the nearby river," the old woman replied.

"How curious. I would like to meet those

swans," Eliza said. "Please tell me where I may find the river."

Eliza followed the path the old woman pointed to and walked along the river until she came to the open sea. There was no further path to follow. There was no boat she could take, no raft on which she could paddle. Eliza was just about to give up when she noticed something caught in the seaweed on the shore. It was eleven white swan feathers.

Eliza gathered up the feathers and placed them together. The feathers glistened in the sunlight, with dewdrops—or tears, Eliza couldn't tell—clinging to their tips.

"It is a sign of some sort," Eliza decided. So she sat down by the shore and waited for what might come next.

At sunset, Eliza saw the eleven white swans with golden crowns on their heads flying toward the shore. Each flew behind the other, like one long white ribbon. Frightened at first, Eliza hid behind some bushes. The swans landed close beside her, but did not know she was hiding there.

As soon as the sun disappeared over the water, the swans' feathers fell off. Eleven beautiful princes were revealed. Eliza uttered a sharp cry. Even though they were much changed, she knew them at once. They were her eleven brothers! She sprang into their arms and called each of them by name.

How happy the princes were to see their long-lost little sister! They recognized her even though she had grown so tall and beautiful. They laughed and wept. Then the eldest prince explained how the wicked queen had enchanted them.

"We fly around as wild swans during the day. We are unable to speak as birds. As soon as the sun sinks behind the hills, we become human again and our voices return. We must always be near a resting place before sunset. For if we were flying toward the clouds when we became human again, we would fall from the sky," the eldest prince told her.

"How can you bear it?" Eliza asked, shaking her head in sympathy.

"We have permission to visit our home once a year for eleven days. We fly across the forest to gaze at the palace where our father lives and where we were born. We visit the church where our true mother is buried. And now we have found you, dear sister," her brother added. "We have two more days left in this part of the world, and then we must head back to the far-away land in which we usually live. You must come with us."

"But how?" Eliza asked. "I cannot fly, and you have no boat, or ship, or extra pair of wings for me," she said sadly.

The eleven princes and Eliza thought for a

moment. Then Eliza started to realize what she and her brothers must do.

"We must break the spell our wicked stepmother has placed on you," she said. Eliza spent all night awake, trying to figure out how to do that. But she could not think of a plan.

The next morning, as the sun rose in the sky, the eleven princes turned back into eleven wild swans. They flapped their great wings and took off. They flew in great wide circles until they were far away. All except the youngest swan, who remained behind and laid his head in his sister's lap. They remained that way all day.

When the other princes returned that evening, they were all sad. "Will you come with us, Eliza?" the youngest swan asked.

"We leave tomorrow for another year. But we can't bear to leave without you. Are you brave enough to go with us?" the eldest asked.

"Yes, take me with you," Eliza agreed. The

brothers cheered up and began preparing for their flight.

They spent the whole night weaving a net of willow reeds. It was very large and very strong. Eliza lay on the net. When the sun rose and her brothers became wild swans again, they took up the net in their beaks. They flew to the clouds, holding up their dear sister, who was still asleep.

Eliza awoke to find herself high in the clouds, as if she were in a dream. The youngest swan shaded her from the sun with his wings. Beside her were fruits that the other brothers had picked during the night so she would have something to eat.

The day passed, and the swans flew as fast as they could to reach their land before nightfall. But as the sun began to set, there was no land in sight, only the black inky sea. Eliza knew it was her fault the swans were flying slower than they usually did. She grew frightened as the sun lowered in the sky. Still there was no land upon which the swans could set their feet.

Just as the sun was about to sink beneath the water, a rock—no larger than a seal's head—appeared in the middle of the ocean. At that moment the swans darted down so swiftly that Eliza's head trembled. They landed on the rock just at the moment when the sun disappeared from the sky. Her brothers formed a circle around her and linked their arms together. There was just enough room for all of them, and not any space to spare.

The sea dashed against the rock and sprayed them. They waited there the whole night, holding hands and singing the songs their true mother sang to them when they were children.

In the early dawn, the air became still and calm. At sunrise, the princes became swans again and flew away, lifting Eliza up from the lonely rock.

The world passed below her as she and the swans flew. At last she saw their destination. She admired its blue mountains, its cedar forests, and its cities and palaces.

By nightfall, they arrived at the cave where the eleven swans had been living. "Sleep well and good dreams, sister," the youngest swan told her.

"I will dream of a way to break your spell," Eliza promised.

That night, Eliza dreamed that the old peasant woman who had been out picking berries came to her.

"This is what you must do to break the spell on your brothers," the old woman said. "Collect as many stinging thorns from the forest as you can bear. Weave them into thread and make eleven long-sleeved coats. If you throw these coats over the eleven swans, the spell will be broken. But you must not speak a single word from the time you begin until the time you finish. If you do, the first word you speak will pierce through the hearts of your brothers like a deadly dagger. Their lives hang on your tongue. Remember what I've told you," the peasant woman said.

Eliza awoke that morning with a start. Determined to make the eleven coats, she began to collect the thorns. Their sticky needles pricked her fingers, her hands, and her arms. But she wouldn't say a single word. When her brothers returned in the evening, they were worried that the wicked queen had put a spell on Eliza to make her mute. But she showed them the thorns and the first of the eleven coats. They realized that she was trying to break the spell, and they were grateful.

When Eliza was almost done with the second coat, she heard the blare of a hunter's horn and the barking of hound dogs. Eliza gathered up her bundles of thorns and put them in a safe place.

Suddenly the hunting dogs burst in and surrounded her. In a few minutes, the hunters found her. The most handsome of the hunters was the king of the country they were in. He came toward her with a smile. She was the most beautiful young woman he had ever seen.

"How did you get here, my dear?" the king asked. Eliza would not answer. She did not want to risk her brothers' lives.

"Come with me," the good, kind king said. "If you are as good as you are beautiful, I will dress you in silk and velvet, and place a golden crown upon your head. And you shall live with me, happily, and rule beside me for all of my days." The king lifted up Eliza and took him with her.

Eliza wept and wrung her hands, but the king did not understand her distress. "I wish only for your happiness," he explained. "Someday you will thank me."

At the king's palace, Eliza allowed the women to dress her in royal robes, weave pearls into her hair, and put soft gloves over her blistered fingers.

When Eliza was presented to the king, he declared that he would make her his bride. Even though Eliza was weeping with sadness, and the chancellor warned him that he thought she was a witch, the king ordered an engagement festival to take place.

After the festival, the king brought Eliza to her own separate room. And there were her bundles of thorns and thread. When Eliza saw these things, she began to smile. The blood rushed to her cheeks. She would be able to break the spell and save her brothers after all! She was so happy she kissed the king's hand, and he pressed her head to his heart. Yet she would not utter a single word.

Meanwhile, the chancellor was still trying to convince the king that Eliza was a witch. But the wise king would not listen. Each night, Eliza secretly left the palace to roam the surrounding grounds and churchyard to collect the rough thorns she needed to make the coats for her brothers.

The chancellor saw Eliza roaming the churchyard. It looked suspicious to him. "I knew she was a witch," he said to himself. "I must convince the king not to marry her."

At first the king would not believe the chancellor. He decided to stay awake that night and watch to see what his beloved was up to.

Sure enough, that night Eliza crept out of the palace and onto the grounds and the churchyard to collect all the thorns she could find. Tears filled the king's eyes.

As night after night passed, the king grew angry with Eliza's actions. Eliza was alarmed by his anger. She did not understand why the king had such a change of heart about her. But she still wanted to save her brothers above all else. So she wove as fast as she possibly could to complete the eleven coats.

Before she was done, the chancellor convinced the king that Eliza was a witch, guilty of robbing the grounds and the churchyard. Eliza was unable to speak a word in her own defense.

Soon the people of the land were calling for Eliza's imprisonment. The king had no choice but to place her in jail.

When she arrived, to her great joy and surprise, her piles of thorns and thread were there. Eliza didn't care that she was to be tried as a witch as long as she got the chance to complete her brothers' coats in time.

At Eliza's trial, they found her guilty. Her execution date was chosen, and it quickly came. The day before, the king visited to plead with her.

"Please tell me you are innocent," he said. But Eliza would not say one word. Later that day, the youngest of the swan brothers found Eliza in her chamber.

"At last, I have found you," he said, flapping his white wings. "We have been looking for you for so long! I must go tell the others."

Soon all the swan brothers came to visit Eliza in her cell. At that moment, Eliza's joy could not have been greater. Just as the sun began to set, she threw the coats onto her brothers' wings. Instantly the spell was broken. However, Eliza had not had time to complete her youngest brother's coat. His left arm remained a wing. All the other princes stood before her, whole and human once again.

"We will find a way to save you, Eliza," they promised. Then the eleven princes, who were swans no longer, kissed her good-bye, promising to return soon.

The next day, when Eliza was brought before the crowd, the king asked her again to tell him that she was innocent. He did not want to believe his adviser's accusations.

"She does not speak in her own defense," the royal adviser said. "Of course she is guilty."

But this time, to everyone's surprise, Eliza stepped forward and spoke in a voice for all to hear. "Your Highness. At very long last, I am able to speak. I tell you the truth. I am innocent."

Just then her eleven brothers stepped forward. "It's true, Your Highness," they said together. They began to explain.

When the crowd heard the story, they bowed to Eliza as though she were a saint. But at that moment Eliza fainted, exhausted from it all.

While the brothers explained all Eliza had done, the fragrance of a million roses filled the air. Instantly a hedge began to blossom with roses, more beautiful and perfect than any that had ever grown before. The king plucked the largest and most beautiful of these flowers and placed it on Eliza's heart. She awoke with a feeling of peace and happiness.

That very day, Eliza and the king were wed. Church bells rang merrily all across the land.

The wicked queen and Eliza's father were never heard from or seen again. And Eliza, the king, and her eleven brothers lived happily ever after.

# Dog Stories

# CHAPTER 9

# A Dog's Tale, by Mark Twain

My father was a St. Bernard dog. My mother was a collie. I'm a Presbyterian. This is what my mother told me. I'm not quite sure what big words like that mean. But my mother liked to say them. She liked to see the looks of surprise and envy on the other dogs' faces. They wondered how she got so smart. But it was only for show.

Mother liked to listen in on people conversations whenever our people had company. Mother also went to Sunday school with the

children, and she learned a lot of big words there. She would repeat words to herself, over and over. She would carry them around in her head like precious jewels. Then, when there was a big dog gathering, she would surprise everyone with a new big word. The dogs who knew her were proud of her vocabulary. The ones who didn't know her were always surprised by her big words. It made them feel small and embarrassed that they didn't understand what she said. When they asked her what the big words meant, she always had an answer.

The other dogs were so impressed with Mother's education, they never doubted what she told them. Perhaps it was because she spoke as though she were reading from the dictionary. Perhaps it was because they had no way of checking whether she was right or wrong. After all, she was the only educated dog they knew.

I believed her, too. That was, until the week when she used the word "unintellectual" at eight different dog gatherings. When asked what it meant, she gave eight different answers. I said nothing, of course. But it did make me doubt how educated Mother really was.

There was one word she always used, like a life preserver. It was kind of an emergency word, for times when conversations took a turn for the terrible or someone dared to doubt her. Mother's emergency word was "synonymous." She could always count on this word to catch a new dog off guard and make him speechless.

For example, if some curious dog asked Mother what something meant and she didn't want to tell him exactly, she would instead reply, "It's synonymous with supererogation." I don't know what it means, either.

After speaking some long word like that, Mother would go about her business, dropping big words here and there. Then the curious dog would slink off, embarrassed, while Mother's crowd of admirers would wag their tails and grin with joy.

It was the same with phrases. Mother would drag home a whole phrase. If it had a grand sound, she would use it every day for six days, sometimes twice on Sundays. She would give it a different meaning every time she used it. Mother never cared about the true meanings of phrases. It just amused her to use them and have the other dogs ask her to explain.

Mother went so far as to recount whole

stories and jokes that she learned from people. The only problem was that Mother never got the whole thing quite right. As she told the story or joke, she would leave things out. The story never quite fit together. At the end of it, she would roll on the floor with laughter even if she couldn't remember why it was so funny. The other dogs would imitate her and roll on the floor with laughter, too. But they were secretly ashamed of themselves for not understanding the joke or story. Little did they know that the fault was not with them but with Mother's bad storytelling.

You can probably see by now that Mother was a bit proud and silly. She had her good points, though. She had a kind heart and gentle ways. She never held a grudge and forgave everyone easily. She taught her children to be kind. We also learned from her to be brave and quick. She showed us how to face danger, not only danger to us but also to friends and family. As you can see, there was more to Mother than just her education.

My time with Mother, however, was not long enough. When I grew up, I was sold and moved away from her. She was brokenhearted. So was I. We cried and cried. She tried to comfort me as best she could.

"We were sent into this world for a wise and good purpose," she told me. "We must do our jobs. Take our lives as we find them. Do our best to help others."

Mother said that men who lived in this way received rewards in another world. We animals could not go to that other world, she explained. But if we always did the right thing, even without a reward, our lives would be worthy. And that was reward enough for us.

Mother had formed these thoughts from when she'd gone to Sunday school with the children. She had studied them well, for our good and for hers. Mother had a wise and thoughtful spirit, in spite of her pride.

As we said good-bye, Mother said to me, through her tears, "Remember, my pup. When there is danger, don't think only of yourself. Think of me and what I would do. Let that be your guide." Do you think I could forget her words? I could not.

After that, I never saw Mother again. I was driven a long, long way from the only place I knew as home. I arrived at a fine house. It was charming, with pictures, decorations, and beautiful furniture. Sunlight flooded every room. There was a lovely garden with many flowers and trees. I became a member of the family at once. They loved me and petted me. They kept my old name, instead of giving me a new one. My name was very dear to me, as it was given to me by my mother: Aileen Mavourneen. She got it from a song. It was a beautiful name, I thought, and so did the Grays, my new family.

Mrs. Gray was thirty, and so sweet and lovely. Sadie was ten and just like her mother. She had auburn hair in pigtails that trailed down her back. The baby was a year old, plump and dimpled. He was so fond of me. The baby pulled my tail and hugged me all day long, laughing as he did it.

Mr. Gray was thirty-eight. He was tall, slender, and handsome. He was a little bald in front, business-like, and focused. His features were perfect. His eyes sparkled with intelligence. He was a renowned scientist. I don't know what that means. But, oh, my mother would have happily shown off that word in front of the other dogs. They would have felt so sad to be so uneducated. The best word, though, is "laboratory." My mother could have saddened all the dogs with that one.

"Laboratory" was not a book, or a picture, or

a place to wash your hands (like "lavatory"). The laboratory was quite different. It was filled with jars, bottles, and electrical things. Every week another scientist came and sat with the master. They used the machines, talked, did experiments, and made discoveries.

Often I came along and stood around listening. I tried to learn, for my mother's sake. In loving memory of her, I tried to understand what the people were saying. It pained me that Mother was missing all this learning and that I didn't understand a bit of it.

Other times I lay on the floor in my mistress's workroom and slept. She gently used me as a footstool, which I loved. Other times I spent hours in the nursery. Sometimes I played with the baby. Sometimes I stood guard over him. Sometimes I would run and play in the beautiful garden with Sadie, until we were both tired. I'd nap in the shade of the biggest tree.

Or sometimes I would visit with the neighbor dogs. There was one dog who was handsome and courteous and very graceful. He was a curly-haired Irish setter named Robin Adair, who was a Presbyterian, just like me!

The servants in our house were all kind to me and were very fond of me. So, as you can see, I led a pleasant life. I was the happiest and most grateful dog in the world. As I had promised my mother, I tried always to do what was right, to honor her memory and her teachings. I wanted to make sure I deserved the happiness that had come to me.

Then one day, my little puppy was born. I was now a mother! My heart was full and my happiness was complete. My puppy was the dearest little thing. His fur was smooth and soft and velvety. He had such little awkward paws, such loving eyes, and such a sweet and inno-cent face. It made me so proud to see how the children and their mother adored it. Yes . . . it seemed to me that life was just too lovely.

Then winter came.

One day, I was standing watch in the nursery (actually I was asleep on the bed beside the baby's crib, but I was still standing watch). The fireplace beside the crib had made the room warm and cozy, so we both slept very soundly. Now, the baby's crib had a tent made of gauzy stuff that you could see through. The baby's nurse was out of the room. The baby and I were alone in the nursery.

A spark from the wood fireplace caught on the gauzy stuff above the crib. The baby's screams woke me. I saw the flames from the crib reaching up to the ceiling. I sprang to the floor and was halfway out the door when I remembered my mother's words. I turned back into the room, reached my head through the flames into the crib, and dragged the baby out by his waistband.

We fell to the floor together in a cloud of smoke. I grabbed him again and dragged the screaming little creature out the door into the hall. I was tugging away, excited and happy and proud that I had saved the baby's life. That's when I heard the master shout.

"Get away from him, you horrible beast!" he cried.

The master's yelling scared me and I stumbled backward to get away from him. When I turned to run away, I twisted my left foreleg. The pain was terrible, but I kept running.

"The nursery's on fire!" the nurse screamed.

The master rushed away. I limped on three legs to the other end of the hall. There was a dark little stairway that led up to an attic where old boxes were kept, and people rarely went.

I climbed up there and searched through all the dark piles. I hid in the most secret place I could find. I was afraid, even though I knew the

master could not see or hear me. I was too afraid to whimper, even though it might have been a comfort. At least I could lick my leg, and that made me feel a little better.

For half an hour there was a lot of noise downstairs—shouting and rushing footsteps. Then there was quiet again for some time, and I was grateful. My fears began to go away. I was happy for this, for fears are far worse than pain. Then I heard a sound that froze my heart. They were calling me. They were shouting my name. They were searching for me!

Their voices were muffled and far away. But still, I was terrified. I heard them calling everywhere—along the halls, through all the rooms, in the basement and the cellar. Also outside, farther and farther away, then back in the house all over again. I thought it would never stop. After hours and hours, the house grew quiet. There was only darkness, black as pitch, in the attic. I was no longer so very afraid. I fell soundly asleep soon after.

I awoke a few hours later. My leg didn't hurt as much as it had before. So I came up with a plan to escape from the attic. I would creep down the back stairs and hide behind the cellar door. When the iceman came at dawn, I would slip out while he was filling the refrigerator with ice. Then I would hide all during the day, and start on my escape when it was night. I didn't know where I would go, but I knew I never wanted to go back to my master. I was quite pleased with my plan, until I had another thought: What would my life be without my dear puppy?

At that thought, my whole plan fell apart. I saw, at once, that I must stay where I was. I would stay and wait and take whatever the master would do to me. I could not leave my puppy. Just then the calling started again. All my sorrows came back. I did not know what I had done to make the master so angry. But I knew whatever it was, he would never forgive me.

The people called my name for what seemed like days and nights. I was so hungry and thirsty. I was getting very weak, and I slept a lot of the time. Once I woke up in a terrible fright. It sounded as if the calling was right in the attic. And it was. It was a child's voice. It was Sadie. The poor thing was crying. My name fell from her lips all broken. I could not believe my ears when I heard what Sadie was saying.

"Come back to us, oh please come back to us. Forgive us. It's too, too sad without you . . ."

I interrupted her with such a grateful little yelp. The next moment, Sadie stumbled through the darkness. She shouted for her family, "She's here! Come to the attic—she's here!"

The days that followed were wonderful. Mrs. Gray, Sadie, and the servants all seemed to worship me. They couldn't do enough for me. They made the finest bed for me. They cooked the most delicious meals for me. Every day friends and neighbors came to hear the story of my heroism (that was what they called it, and it means farming, I'm sure).

A dozen times a day Mrs. Gray and Sadie would tell the tale to visitors. They would say I risked my life to save the baby's. Then the visitors would pass me around, petting and adoring me. I could see the pride in Sadie's and her mother's eyes. When the people wanted to know what made me limp, Sadie and her mother looked ashamed and changed the subject. It looked as though they were going to cry.

There was even more glory than this! The master's friends came. Twenty of the most important people. They took me into the laboratory and discussed me as if I were an exciting discovery. Some said I was a wonderful dumb beast who had shown fine survival instincts.

My master argued that I had acted far beyond that. I had used *reason,* and far better reason than many men he knew, including himself.

"I thought the dog had gone mad and was destroying the child," he said with a bitter laugh. "But without this dog's intelligence and ability to reason, the baby would have died."

Master and his friends argued the point for quite some time. I just wished my mother could have known the grand honor that was mine. It would have made her proud.

# CHAPTER 10

# Brown Wolf, by Jack London

～

Madge Irvine pulled on her shoes and rushed out of the house. "Where's Wolf?" she asked her husband, who was eyeing a bursting almond bud. Madge cast a glance across the tall grass and in and out among the orchard trees.

"He was here a minute ago," Walt Irvine said. "He was running after a rabbit when I saw him last."

"Here, Wolf! Here, boy," Madge called.

She left the clearing and followed the trail that led through the forest to the county road.

Walt gave a shrill, loud whistle. Madge put her hands over her ears to drown out the piercing sound.

"There's Wolf!" she cried happily.

From the thicket-covered hillside forty feet above them, on the edge of a cliff, Wolf's head and shoulders came crashing out of the underbrush. He gazed below at the man and the woman, his mouth open. He looked like he was smiling at them.

"You blessed Wolf!" they called up to him.

His ears flattened back and down at the sound of their voices, as if to snuggle under an invisible hand.

They walked up and met him along the trail. He did not require much petting. A pat and a rub around the ears from the man. A longer stroke from the woman. Then he was on his way along the trail, gliding in front of them in true wolf fashion.

He looked like a huge wolf with his thick coat and large build. But he had the unmistakable coloring of a dog. He was brown. Not just any brown, but a deep brown, a red-brown, a collection of all sorts of browns. His back and shoulders were a warm brown. On the sides he was a pale brown. And his underbelly was a yellow, dingy brown. There was white fur at his throat and paws, and white spots surrounded his golden-brown eyes.

The man and the woman loved the dog very much. It had been very hard for them to win his love. Wolf had drifted into their lives mysteriously, from nowhere to their little mountain cottage. Nearly starving, he had killed a rabbit right under their window. Then he crawled away and slept by a small spring at the foot of their blackberry bushes. When Walt Irvine had gone down to see the dog, Wolf had snarled at him. When Madge Irvine offered him bread and a pan of milk, he snarled at her, too.

For a long time, Wolf refused their kindness. He wouldn't let them pet him. He threatened them with his bare fangs. Nevertheless, he stayed beside their spring, resting and eating the food they brought him. After several days, when he was feeling and looking better, he disappeared. This could have been the end of the relationship among Madge, Walt, and the dog.

But then Walt was called away to work, and while traveling on the train he looked out the window and saw Wolf running alongside. He was tireless, dust-covered, and two hundred miles away from Walt's mountain cottage!

Without thinking, Walt hopped off the train at the next station and bought a piece of meat at a butcher shop. He enticed the dog with the meat, captured him, and traveled with him in the baggage car. He brought him back to the mountain cottage.

Walt and Madge tied up Wolf so that he could not escape. They spent the next week giving him as much love and attention as they could. Wolf snarled at their soft-spoken words. He growled at their attempts to pet him. He never barked, though. In all the time they knew him, he never once barked.

Winning Wolf's affections was a problem. But Walt Irvine liked problems. He made a collar with a silver plate that read, RETURN TO WALT IRVINE, SONOMA COUNTY, CA.

Then Walt let Wolf loose. And again—Wolf

disappeared! He made it more than a hundred miles up to Oregon before Walt received a telegram telling him that Wolf had been captured. The dog went back by Wells Fargo Express that evening, and the couple tied him up for three more days. On the fourth day when Walt let him loose, he disappeared. Again, Walt got a call that someone had captured Wolf. This time, he got farther north. Wolf always headed north. "Some kind of instinct, I guess," Walt said to Madge.

The next time Wolf wandered off, he made it all the way up past California, Oregon, and halfway into Washington State. Again, someone picked him up and returned him to the Irvines.

Wolf traveled with remarkable speed. On a one-day run he could travel close to 150 miles, Walt figured. But no matter how far Wolf got, when he was brought back, he was always lean, hungry, and wild. He always left when he was fresh and strong again. And he always headed north, although no one understood why.

After one last time running away, Wolf accepted his fate. He stayed at the mountain cottage with Walt and Madge. It took another several weeks before Wolf would allow Madge and Walt, and only them, to pet him. Wolf never cared much for strangers. If anyone dared to come near him, they were greeted with a low growl, which quickly became a snarl. He had a snarl so terrible and deadly looking that it frightened the bravest of men and dogs.

Wolf had no history. His life began and ended with Walt and Madge. He had come up from the south, but that's all they knew. Mrs. Johnson, the Irvines' nearest neighbor, called Wolf a Klondike dog. She was an authority on the frozen part of the country called the Klondike. Her brother was working up there and sent her regular letters about it.

Walt and Madge agreed with Mrs. Johnson. It looked like the tips of Wolf's ears had been severely frozen at one time and never healed right. He looked like those dogs they saw in magazines about Alaska. They spent many afternoons trying to imagine a past for Wolf. At night, they would hear him crying softly. When the north wind blew and there was the bite of frost in the air, Wolf became restless. He would lift his head and give a long howl. It was so sad and so lonely that it gave them goose bumps. Yet he never barked. Never.

Walt and Madge would half argue about whose dog Wolf really was, his or hers. Walt was sure that Wolf cared more for him. After all, what did Wolf know about women? The swish of Madge's skirts made him shudder.

On the other hand, Madge was the one who fed him. She ruled the kitchen, and only with her permission was he allowed to enter it. Walt claimed that Wolf would lie at his feet when he was writing. He said he spent more time petting Wolf than he did getting any writing done.

In the end, Walt won. But Madge insisted that if Walt had actually been writing, Wolf would have probably spent more time with her.

So, one lovely day, Walt and Madge were on their way to the post office. Walt was going to mail off another piece of writing and pick up a check for his last one. Just then, a large and strong-looking man, sweating in his tight-fitting black suit, greeted them along the road.

"I'm looking for my sister, Mrs. Johnson," the stranger said. "Do you know her?"

"You're her Klondike brother!" Madge exclaimed.

"The name's Skiff Miller. Thought I'd just up and surprise her by coming to visit," he said.

So Madge and Walt directed Mrs. Johnson's brother to the trail that led to her house. But

Skiff Miller was staring. He was so taken with Madge's beauty that he was unable to move. Just as Walt decided it was time for him to send this Skiff on his way, Wolf trotted toward them.

Skiff's expression changed immediately. He was no longer interested in Madge. He had eyes only for the dog. Great wonder washed over his face.

"Well, I'll be darned," he said slowly. Then he sat down with a heavy thump on a nearby log.

At the sound of Skiff's voice, Wolf's ears flattened. His mouth opened in a laugh. He trotted slowly to the stranger and smelled his hands, then licked them with his tongue.

Skiff Miller patted the dog's head. Slowly and solemnly he repeated his words, "Well, I'll be darned." Then he remembered the pretty woman beside him. "Sorry, ma'am. I'm just mighty surprised."

"We're surprised, too," Madge said. "We've never seen Wolf act so kindly to a stranger."

"Is that what you call him? Wolf?" Skiff Miller asked.

Madge nodded. "But I can't understand this. Unless it's because he's a Klondike dog and somehow he knows you're from the Klondike."

Skiff Miller lifted one of Wolf's forelegs and examined the paw pads. He pressed them and dented them with his thumb. "Kind of soft," he remarked. "He hasn't been on the trail for a long time."

"It is quite remarkable how he allows you to touch him," Walt exclaimed.

Skiff Miller stood up abruptly, completely forgetting about Madge. In a sharp and business-like tone he asked, "How long have you had him?"

Just then, Wolf rubbed against Skiff's legs. Then the dog opened his mouth and barked! It was loud, sharp bark—brief and full of joy.

Walt and Madge stared at each other. The miracle had happened. Wolf had barked.

"It's the first time he's ever barked," Walt explained.

"First time I ever heard him bark, too," Skiff said.

"'Course it is," Madge said with a smile. "You've only known him for five minutes."

Skiff Miller gave Madge a funny look. "I thought you understood," he said slowly. "This is my dog. His name isn't Wolf. It's Brown."

"Oh, Walt!" Madge said in dismay, grabbing her husband's arm.

"How do you know he's your dog?" Walt demanded.

"Because he is," Skiff replied.

"You don't know that for sure," Walt said.

Skiff gazed at Walt and Madge for a moment. "Look. The dog's mine. I raised him from when he was a pup. See. I'll prove it to you." Then Skiff turned to the dog and said, "Brown! Gee! Turn to the right!"

The dog made a swinging turn to the right.

"Now mush-on!" Skiff's voice rang out.

The dog stopped turning and started moving straight ahead.

"Brown, halt!" Skiff commanded. The dog stopped immediately.

"I can even make him follow with whistles," Skiff said proudly. "He was my lead sled dog."

"But you can't take him away," Madge said. "Not back to that awful Klondike world of suffering."

"I am," Skiff Miller said. Then he added, "It's not as bad as all that, though. Look at me. I'm fit as a fiddle."

"But it's an awful life for dogs. Backbreaking work, starvation, frost! I've read about it. I know!" Madge said.

"Brown knows that life. He likes it. He's used

to it. He was born and brought up in it. That's where the dog belongs, and that's where he'll be happiest."

"The dog does not go," Walt said in a stern voice. "Just because he obeys the ordinary commands of the Alaskan trail doesn't mean he's yours. He's probably valuable and that's why you want him. You haven't proven that he belongs to you, and you can't take him."

Skiff Miller looked Walt up and down. His face flushed with anger. His muscles bulged under the black cloth of his suit. He eyed the thin writer and said in a threatening voice, "There's nothing in sight that can keep me from taking the dog right here and now."

Walt's face, too, reddened in anger. His shoulders went up and he balled his hands into fists.

"Maybe Mr. Miller is right," Madge said. "Wolf does seem to know him. And the dog does answer to the name 'Brown.' They made friends instantly, and Wolf never does that. Besides, he barked. With joy! Because he had found Mr. Miller again," Madge told Walter.

Walter's hands dropped and his shoulders drooped with hopelessness.

"I guess you're right, Madge," Walt agreed.

"Perhaps we can buy him?" Madge asked Skiff hopefully.

"I had five dogs," Skiff said, trying to find a nice way to turn down Madge's offer. "Brown was the leader. They were the best team in Alaska. Nothing could touch them. I said no to the last person who offered me five thousand dollars for them. Brown is the best on my team. I said no to twelve hundred dollars that was offered just for him. I wouldn't sell him then, and I won't sell him now. I've been looking for him for three years. I was sad when he was stolen from me. And I couldn't believe my eyes when I saw him just now. I thought I was dreaming. Thought it was too good to be true. I was his master. I put him to bed every night. He was just a pup when his mother died. I brought him up on condensed milk in a can when I couldn't afford my own coffee. Brown never knew any mother but me," Skiff told them, looking like he might cry.

"But what about what's best for the dog?" Madge said.

"What do you mean?" Skiff asked.

"Perhaps the dog prefers California to Alaska. Did you ever consider that?" Madge asked. "If you really love him, you should do what would make the dog happiest. You shouldn't simply choose a hard life for him because it suits you."

Skiff Miller considered what Madge had said. Madge and Walt exchanged a look.

"Well, he was a really good worker. And he's got a good head on him. He can do everything but talk. He knows what you say to him. Look—he knows we're talking about him right now," said Skiff, pointing to the dog. Madge and Walt looked at Wolf.

The dog was lying at Skiff's feet, his head close down on his paws, ears up. His eyes were quick, listening to each of them as they spoke.

"And there's a lot of work left in him," Skiff added. Then he looked at the dog. Skiff opened and closed his mouth several times, as if not sure of what to say next. Finally, he spoke.

"I'll tell you what, ma'am," Skiff began. "The dog's worked hard. He's earned his right to choose. We'll leave it up to him. Whatever he says goes. You people stay right here sitting down. I'll say good-bye and walk off real casually. If the dog wants to stay, he can stay. If he wants to come with me, let him come. I won't call him to come to me. You don't call him to come to you."

Then Skiff peered hard into Madge's face. "Now, play fair. No waving to him to come to you once my back is turned," he warned.

"We'll play fair," Madge promised.

"Well, then. I guess I might as well be getting along," Skiff said. At the change of tone in Skiff's voice, Wolf lifted his head. As Madge and Skiff shook hands, Wolf sprang up on his hind legs, resting his front paws on Madge's hip while licking Skiff Miller's hand. Then Skiff shook hands with Walt, and Wolf did the same thing again.

With a long, sad sigh, Skiff turned away and began to walk slowly along the path to Mrs. Johnson's house.

For twenty feet, Wolf watched him go, expecting at any moment for Skiff to turn around and return. Then, with a quick low whine, the dog sprang after him and gently took Skiff's hand in his mouth to make him stop.

Skiff kept on going. Wolf raced back to where Walt sat. He caught Walt's coat sleeve in his teeth and tried to drag him after Skiff.

Wolf became more and more upset. He wanted to be in two places at the same time, with the old master and the new ones. He ran about, going back and forth between them in short nervous leaps and twists. He was unable to choose, and he uttered quick, sharp whines.

Wolf sat down on his hind legs. He raised his head in the air, about to let out a long, loud howl. But before he did, he closed his mouth and looked long and steadily at Skiff's back. Then he turned his head and looked directly into Walt's eyes. Neither Walt nor Skiff gave the dog a sign or a clue as to what he should do.

As Skiff began to disappear around a bend in the trail, the dog looked over at Madge. He went over to her. He snuggled his head into her lap, nudging her arm with his nose. Then he backed away from her, twisting playfully on the ground at her feet. He was trying to get someone to tell him what he should do. But none of the humans would respond at all.

He turned and silently gazed after Skiff. In a moment the man would be gone from view. Skiff never turned his head to see what was happening behind his back. When Skiff disappeared around the bend, Wolf waited for him to reappear. He waited and waited and waited. He barked once. Then waited some more. It was as if the dog had turned to stone.

Finally, he turned and trotted back to Walt. He sniffed Walt's hand and dropped down heavily at his feet. He kept watching the trail where Skiff had disappeared from view.

A tiny stream gurgled nearby. Meadowlarks chirped. There was no other sound. Great yellow butterflies darted silently through the slices of sunshine and shadows. Madge gazed in victory at Walt.

A few minutes later Wolf stood up. He did not glance at the man and woman. His eyes were fixed upon the trail. He had made up his mind. They knew it.

The dog broke into a trot. Madge tensed her lips to make the whistling sound she used to call Wolf to her. Walt gave her a stern look. Madge did not whistle.

Wolf broke into a run. Wider and wider he leaped along the trail. He did not turn his head once to look at Madge and Walt. His wolf's tail stood out straight behind him. He cut sharply across the curve of the trail.

And in an instant, Wolf was gone.

# Stories from
# "Queer Little Folks"

*by Harriet Beecher Stowe*

༄

# CHAPTER 11

# The Squirrels That Live in a House

◦

Once upon a time, an elderly gentleman went out into a great forest. He cut away the trees and built a very nice little retirement cottage for him and his wife. It had very large windows. The windows were so large that the gentleman could see through on every side and know what was going on in the forest.

He could see the shadows of the fern leaves as they shifted over the ground. He could see the red partridgeberries and winter-green plums that fell to the ground beside the trees. He could see the bright spots of sunshine that fell through the branches. He could see the chirping sparrows, robins, and bluebirds building their nests. He watched them as they laid their eggs and hatched their young.

He could also see the red squirrels, gray squirrels, and little striped chip-squirrels scampering around the forest. They raced one another from tree limb to tree limb. They chattered happily with one another all day long.

Now, a house for a human was a strange thing for all the creatures in the wood. They were very curious about it. While it was being built, the older forest creatures felt very disturbed. Every creature had an opinion about what they thought was going on.

Old Mrs. Rabbit declared that the hammering and pounding made her nervous. She predicted evil times ahead. "Be sure of it, children," she warned her long-eared little ones. "No good will come to us from this cottage building. Wherever humans are, there is trouble for us rabbits."

The squirrels that lived in the old chestnut tree were also quite sure that the new cottage spelled trouble for them all.

"It's clear that the humans will spoil everything for us. They will take all the nuts from our tree and use them for themselves," warned old Father Gray Squirrel.

Old Ground-Mole had to agree. "It will bring down the value of our homes in the forest," he declared. "Every decent-minded creature will want to move away now that the humans are here. I know that's what I will do."

The bluebirds and bobolink birds had more positive thoughts about the humans. But Old Mrs. Ground-Mole remarked that they were a silly bunch of birds. They flew here and there, and were not settled. They could not be expected to understand the forest creatures' attachment to their neighborhood and their opinions were not taken seriously.

"Humans never stop in their war against Nature. They create ruin that would take hundreds of years to repair. Humans can destroy in a few hours what it has taken Nature ages to produce," complained the Old Chestnut Tree.

"I'd like to see the best of the humans create anything as magnificent as the old oak tree," the Chestnut Tree continued. "Who among these foolish humans could make a tree? And the noise they make—it's ridiculous! In the forest, we do everything quietly. A tree would be ashamed if it made even half the noise these humans do while it grew. Our manners are perfect. Humans are rude and selfish," the Chestnut Tree complained.

The little cottage was finished, even with all the disagreement from the forest creatures. Its walls were covered with pretty paper.

Its floors were laid with pretty carpets. Once it was all done, and the garden paths were paved and pretty flowers were planted, even the most doubtful forest creatures changed their minds. The cottage was not so bad after all.

One day a black ant went in and explored the cottage. The ant crawled over chairs and tables. It crawled on walls and ceilings. The ant reported in *The Crickets' Gazette* that the cottage was like a palace on the inside. Several butterflies sailed through the windows and fluttered about. They said the cottage was delightful. Some bees buzzed through and were enchanted by the cottage, especially by its garden.

In fact, it became clear that the humans in this cottage loved Nature as much as the creatures did. The humans watched over and saved the wildflowers and weeds. They watched with great interest as the birds built their nests. They never allowed anything to threaten the creatures around them. Soon enough, every insect and bird and beast in the forest praised the humans.

"Mama," asked Little Bit, a young and curious squirrel, "why won't you let Frisky and me go into that pretty new cottage to play?"

"My dear," said old Mama Squirrel, "humans set many dangerous traps for us creatures. If you had wings like the butterflies and bees, you could safely enter the cottage and leave whenever you wanted. But since you do not, it's best if you keep out of the humans' way."

"But Mama," protested Little Bit. "I have seen the woman who lives in the cottage. She's like a good fairy. She seems to love us creatures. She sits in the big window and watches us for hours. She scatters corn around the tree roots for us to eat."

"She is nice enough, as long as you keep your distance," warned Mama Squirrel. "You can't be too careful around humans."

The "good fairy" who was watching the squirrels was a little old lady all the woodland creatures called Aunt Esther. She dearly loved all animals. Each day she scattered crumbs for the sparrows. She set out little bits of bread and wool and cotton to help the birds build their nests. She tossed out corn and nuts for the squirrels. She sat at her window and would smile and wave at the animals. After a while, the birds grew so comfortable that they would hop onto the window and eat the squirrels' crumbs.

"Look, Mama," said Little Bit and Frisky. "Jenny Wren and Red Robin have been at the window. They didn't get hurt. Can't we go, too? Please!"

"Well, my dears," said Mama Squirrel, not wanting to disappoint her little ones. "If you go, you must be very careful. Remember, you don't have wings like Jenny Wren and Red Robin."

The next day, Aunt Esther laid a path of corn

for the animals. It went from the roots of the trees to her window and from the window to her workbasket, which was on the floor beside her. Then she put a handful of corn in her workbasket. She sat down by the basket and began to work on her sewing. She didn't look around. She concentrated only on the needle and thread in her lap.

Very soon, Frisky and Little Bit came creeping up to the window. Then, as quiet as could be, they crept into the room. Aunt Esther sat as still as a statue. She did not want to frighten the squirrels.

The little squirrels looked around the cottage with delight. When they came to the basket, it seemed like a wonderful thing for them to play in. They put their noses inside it. They turned over the scissors and the packet of needles. They took a nibble at her white thread. They played with spools and thimbles. As they played, they stored the corn bits on either side of their mouths. They both had huge lumps in their cheeks.

Aunt Esther put her hand out to touch them—she couldn't help it. The squirrels ran out the window and up the trees as quickly as they could move. They were up in the branches chattering and laughing before Aunt Esther could even blink.

After that, the two little squirrels visited Aunt Esther every day. Eventually, they felt comfortable enough to eat corn right out of her hand. One day they actually jumped right into her hand. Aunt Esther gently closed her hand over the two squirrels. Frisky and Little Bit were caught!

Their hearts beat fast with fear. But the old woman spoke gently to them. Soon she opened her hand and let them go. Day after day they grew closer to her. They would climb into her workbasket, sit on her shoulder, or snuggle in her lap as she sewed. They made long trips to explore all over the house. The house was amazing. They climbed up the stairs and into all the rooms. And when they returned to the chestnut tree, they told all the other squirrels about their adventures.

Then one winter, the good fairy and the gentleman who had built the house passed away. The squirrels' mother told them that the couple had gone to a land where flowers never fade and birds always sing. The young squirrels continued to go the cottage, their favorite place. A new family had moved in.

"You know, my dear," said Mama Squirrel to her husband. "What is the use of living in this cold, hollow tree when there is a pretty little cottage right next door? There is plenty of room for us and the humans," she went on. "We can store our nuts right below the roof, and be warm and cozy in the winter. And we can move around as we like. We won't even disturb the humans."

So Mr. and Mrs. Squirrel set up house under the roof of the cottage. They stored all their nuts and things up there. However, there was one small problem. Mrs. Squirrel was a busy creature. She woke up early every morning to make sure that all the children were fed, bathed, dressed, and ready for the day. Sometimes, Mrs. Squirrel would scold her poor husband late at night. He would then scurry off to another part of the cottage to get some sleep.

This greatly disturbed the new family that had come to live in the cottage. They did not like the noise the squirrels made during the early mornings and late nights.

But when the good people would look out their windows on a cold winter morning, they saw the squirrels dancing and frisking down the trees. The animals chased each other so merrily over the garden chair between them, or sat with their bold tails swooped over their backs.

The squirrels looked so jolly and pretty that the humans almost forgave them for disturbing their night of rest. Each person secretly thought, "Perhaps I will not do anything to drive the poor creatures out of the attic today."

But how long will the squirrels get to live in the cottage in this way? Well, I suppose it's anyone's guess! What should they do? What would you do? Would you let the squirrels live in your house?

# CHAPTER 12

# Mother Magpie's Mischief

Old Mother Magpie was just about the busiest creature in the forest. But there is a difference between being busy and working hard. You can be very busy but not hardworking at all. This was the case with Mother Magpie.

She was into everybody's business but her own. She was here, there, and everywhere, but never in her own nest. She knew what everyone else was doing. And she had words of advice for every bird and beast in the forest.

One day Mother Magpie flew up to the top

of the oak tree where old Parson Too-Whit lived. She told him exactly how awful everyone in the forest was. "You ought to scold all the badly behaving creatures in next Sunday's sermon," she said.

Then she left the old gentleman in a dazed and confused state and peeped into Mrs. Oriole's nest. Mother Magpie chattered so much to Mrs. Oriole that she was more bewildered than if a terrible wind had shook her.

"Believe me, my dear," Mother Magpie cheeped, "this is no way to build a nest. It swings in the air like an empty stocking. I never built a nest like this one, and I never had a single problem with my nests. You complain of a headache whenever I visit. It's on account of the way your nest swings in the air, I do declare," Mother Magpie told her as she puffed out her chest.

"Orioles always build their nests this way,"

Mrs. Oriole softly said. Mother Magpie made her feel shy.

"Fiddlesticks!" said Mother Magpie. "You'll never learn if you never try. Just ask Dr. Kite— he agrees with me. Have you ever been to any of Dr. Kite's lectures?"

"No. I can't leave my eggs," Mrs. Oriole explained.

"Nonsense! Let your husband sit on the eggs," Mother Magpie advised. "He should sit on them half the time to give you a chance to move around and exercise. My husband does this for me. I shall have to speak to yours," Mother Magpie said.

"Oh, please do not," said Mrs. Oriole.

"We'll see about that," Mother Magpie said, and flew off in a huff.

Later that day, when Tommy Oriole returned to the nest, he was very upset.

"Have you been gossiping about me, your husband, to Mother Magpie?" he asked Mrs. Oriole.

"She simply will not leave me be," Mrs. Oriole declared. "I don't say a word and she insists on giving me advice. She thinks you should mind the eggs half the time so I can move around and exercise. Not really a bad idea, if you think about it," Mrs. Oriole dared to say.

"Tell her to mind her own business," Tommy Oriole said. "I am a society bird, and you must learn to live with that, dear wife. Be glad that you have a brilliant and handsome husband, able to sing like an angel. I must attend concerts and spend time around the forest. I cannot simply stay in the nest and warm the eggs. I have very important business," Tommy explained.

Now, Tommy Oriole was very much annoyed with Mother Magpie for butting into his nest life. After all, Mrs. Oriole had never complained about him before Mother Magpie brought him to her attention.

Meanwhile, Mother Magpie was off minding

someone else's business. She went down to Water-Dock Lane to visit the old music teacher, Dr. Bullfrog. The poor old doctor was a simple creature, good and kind. He had led the forest choir for as long as anyone could remember. Lately, however, the forest was no longer a simple place to live. How had the forest changed? Forest animals had always been polite and respectful. But just recently, a number of young and rowdy creatures had tried to interrupt Dr. Bullfrog's forest choir concerts!

That wasn't all. Some of the young rascals had begun gossiping about the good doctor. They made fun of the way he sang in his deep, double bass voice. They refused to be part of the choir, or even go to the concerts. They wanted a new choir leader who would play different and new sorts of music.

Dr. Bullfrog knew nothing about this. He simply went about his business and prepared for the next forest choir concert. That is, until Mother Magpie came to visit.

"Well, Dr. Bullfrog, I hope you know that I think your music is simply wonderful. Young people today know nothing about music! They have no respect for our age group and the way we do things. I think your teaching and singing have never been better. Honestly, these young folks never listen to reasonable folks," Mother Magpie chattered on.

Dr. Bullfrog cleared his throat and said. "I'm afraid I don't understand you, ma'am."

"Do you mean to say you don't know that a group of young rascals is going to ask you to resign from the forest choir? They are already in your choir, plotting and planning!" Mother Magpie shrieked.

"You must be mistaken," Dr. Bullfrog croaked.

Mother Magpie huffed and puffed. "I am

never mistaken, good Doctor," she told him. "I know everything weeks and weeks in advance. Surely you know that," Mother Magpie said, turning to Mrs. Bullfrog.

"Oh, my poor husband," Mrs. Bullfrog groaned. "We shall be ruined!"

"Now, just a minute," Mother Magpie said. "If you take my advice, you may be fine after all. You must change your music style a little. Make it more modern. Include some higher notes, like Tommy Oriole's singing," Mother Magpie suggested.

"Ma'am, I am a bullfrog. Consider my voice. I cannot possibly hit the high notes," Dr. Bullfrog protested.

"Nonsense," Mother Magpie replied. "It's just a matter of practice. Of course your voice is croaky and hoarse. You sit all day long in the cold water. Get out of the water and into the tree branches, like we birds do. Then you'll be

able to sing those high notes with no problem
Trust me."

Against his own wishes, Dr. Bullfrog left his
cottage under the riverbank. He went to the
garden and sat alone on a tree limb to practice his
musical scales. He tried to hit the high notes.

The result was disastrous. Instead of gaining
more respect as a musical gentleman, he found
that every bird and beast in the forest made fun
of him. They all laughed at him for trying to be
something he was not. Even Parson Too-Whit
scolded Dr. Bullfrog for not acting right.

And Mother Magpie? She pretended she had
not advised Dr. Bullfrog at all. She told everyone
how sorry she felt that poor, old Dr. Bullfrog was
acting like such a fool. "He should have taken my
advice and kept on being his old, respectable self,"
Mother Magpie told anyone who would listen.

After that, things went from bad to worse
for Dr. Bullfrog. One day, as he sat under a berry

bush, quietly practicing his usual deep notes, there was a terrible thump! A great garden hoe struck Dr. Bullfrog and nearly broke his back.

"What ugly beast do we have here?" asked Tom Noakes, the gardener's son. "Come here, Wasp. Get him!" Tom called to his dog.

Poor old Dr. Bullfrog was frightened when he saw the dog running toward him. Wasp was barking and yelping. Then, with a strength he didn't know he had, Dr. Bullfrog leaped over a patch of bushes into the river. He swam away as fast as he could, back to his little home beneath the riverbank.

From that day on, Dr. Bullfrog never listened to any more gossip or advice from anyone, especially from Mother Magpie. And he called her Old Mother Mischief whenever he thought of her, which he tried never to do at all.

# What Do *You* Think?
## Questions for Discussion

∽

Have you ever been around a toddler who keeps asking the question "Why?" Does your teacher call on you in class with questions from your homework? Do your parents ask you questions about your day at the dinner table? We are always surrounded by questions that need a specific response. But is it possible to have a question with no right answer?

The following questions are about the book you just read. But this is not a quiz! They are designed to help you look at the people, places, and events in the stories from different angles. These questions do not have specific answers. Instead, they might make you think of the stories in a completely new way.

Think carefully about each question and enjoy discovering more about these classic stories.

1. In the stories that you have read, the animals are the main characters. Can you think of an animal you know that could tell a story? What would that story be about?

2. Do you think each of the animals in Kipling's "Just So" Stories get what he or she deserves? What would it be like if the Elephant got the hump, the Camel got the spots, and the Leopard got the long trunk?

3. Eliza, the sister of "The Wild Swans," finds herself in a difficult situation. If you were in Eliza's shoes, would you speak up to save your

own life or choose to be silent and save your brothers?

4. How might the outcome of the story "The Leap-Frog" be different if the animals raced in a different kind of competition, like a singing contest or contest of strength? What kind of contest do you think you could easily win?

5. In the same story, the King declares to the crowd "A contest is only as good as its reward." If you were creating a special contest, what would be the prize? Have you ever competed and won the grand prize?

6. In "A Dog's Tale," the main character, Aileen Mavourneen, talks lovingly about her mother and all the funny things she says. If you were to rewrite the beginning of this story, what might you write about one of your parents? What funny things do your parents say?

7. The Grays treat Aileen as part of the family. Do you have a pet that is like part of your

family? How do you make your pet feel comfortable and welcome?

8. In the story "Brown Wolf," do you think Wolf made the right decision at the end? If you were Wolf, who would you decide to stay with?

9. The story "The Squirrels that Live in the House" ends with the question "Would you let the squirrels live in your house?" Well, would you? What might be fun about having them stay? What might be bad?

10. Do you agree with the name Dr. Bullfrog gave Mother Magpie: Old Mother Mischief? Do you know anyone in real life who is like Mother Magpie?

# A Note to Parents and Educators
*By Arthur Pober, EdD*

⁓

First impressions are important.

Whether we are meeting new people, going to new places, or picking up a book unknown to us, first impressions count for a lot. They can lead to warm, lasting memories or can make us shy away from any future encounters.

Can you recall your own first impressions and earliest memories of reading the classics?

Do you remember wading through pages and pages of text to prepare for an exam? Or were you the child who hid under the blanket to read with a flashlight, joining forces with Robin Hood to save Maid Marian? Do you remember only how long it took you to read a lengthy novel such as *Little Women*? Or did you become best friends with the March sisters?

Even for a gifted young reader, getting through long chapters with dense language can easily become overwhelming and can obscure the richness of the story and its characters. Reading an abridged, newly crafted version of a classic novel can be the gentle introduction a child needs to explore the characters and story-line without the frustration of difficult vocabulary and complex themes.

Reading an abridged version of a classic novel gives the young reader a sense of independence and the satisfaction of finishing a "grown-up" book. And when a child is engaged with and inspired by a classic story, the tone is set for further exploration of the story's themes, characters, history, and details. As a child's reading skills advance, the desire to tackle the original, unabridged version of the story will naturally emerge.

If made accessible to young readers, these stories can become invaluable tools for understanding themselves in the context of their families and social environments. This is why the Classic Starts series includes questions that stimulate discussion regarding the impact and social relevance of the characters and stories today. These questions can foster lively conversations between children and their parents or teachers. When we look at the issues, values, and standards of past times in terms of how we live now, we can appreciate literature's classic tales in a very personal and engaging way.

Share your love of reading the classics with a young child, and introduce an imaginary world real enough to last a lifetime.

## Dr. Arthur Pober, EdD

Dr. Arthur Pober has spent more than twenty years in the fields of early childhood and gifted education. He is the former principal of one of the world's oldest laboratory schools for gifted youngsters, Hunter College Elementary School, and former Director of Magnet Schools for the Gifted and Talented for more than 25,000 youngsters in New York City.

Dr. Pober is a recognized authority in the areas of media and child protection and is currently the U.S. representative to the European Institute for the Media and European Advertising Standards Alliance.

Explore these wonderful stories in our
Classic Starts™ library.

*Pinocchio*

*Pollyanna*

*The Prince and the Pauper*

*Rebecca of Sunnybrook Farm*

*The Red Badge of Courage*

*Robinson Crusoe*

*The Secret Garden*

*The Story of King Arthur and His Knights*

*The Strange Case of Dr. Jekyll and Mr. Hyde*

*The Swiss Family Robinson*

*The Three Musketeers*

*The Time Machine*

*Treasure Island*

*The Voyages of Doctor Dolittle*

*The War of the Worlds*

*White Fang*

*The Wind in the Willows*